The Ancient Path

by Dan Rendell

immortalise

THE ANCIENT PATH

Cataloguing-in-Publication entry is available from the National Library of Australia http:/catalogue.nla.gov.au/.

This edition first published in August 2024
Hackham, South Australia.

ISBN paperback   978-0-6459991-4-3
     hardcover   978-0-6459991-6-7
     ebook   978-0-6459991-5-0

Illustrations and cover art by Elena Rogers

Typesetting and cover layout by Ben Morton

Published in Australia by Immortalise via Ingram Spark
www.immortalise.com.au

For my Grandfather, Frank William Rendell,
1941-2024
"The action of a moment can cause a lifetime of regret."

Chapter 1

William's Dilemma

Sometimes, along the path of life, we encounter a fork in the road. Such was the case for William. Having turned eighteen three months earlier, William had finally become a man and could choose a wife.

However, for the past few weeks he'd been torn inside. There were two eligible women in his village, both of whom he was fond of. The first, Mary, had been his friend since childhood. The second, Krystal, was the most beautiful maiden in all the land. Krystal's beauty was known far and wide, and many suitors from surrounding villages had come to court her. Yet, none of them could win her hand.

Krystal was hopeful for a young man who could provide her with a luxurious future, but she also wanted to be romanced—to be swept off her feet. The most handsome man in town was Gregory. His family was wealthy, but he had little interest in romance. William, on the other hand, was a romantic.

William was born and reared Geldirik, an isolated farming community in the far north. The people of Geldirik were known for being stubborn and anti-social, often opposed to change. They had no desire to expand their quaint little village, or venture from it, in search of something different. Krystal, like all who lived in Geldirik, also had no desire to leave. This was William's best hope for winning her hand.

He was deeply fond of his childhood friend, Mary, but like most young men, he had been captivated by Krystal's beauty. His father advised him not to pursue her, but William's father had left the village many months ago. Right now, he was standing on some distant shore, fighting for king and country. William loved his father, but his father's absence had given him the time to woo Krystal with his romantic ideals.

Standing in the centre of town by the old stone archway, William was doing his best to romance her. "Thank you for the rose," she smiled.

"What is a rose compared to your beauty?" he whispered in her ear.

Krystal smiled again. "I wish every man could speak his heart. You always know the right thing to say, but shouldn't you be at work?"

"I left work early to see you," he said, looking deeply into her eyes.

"Does your mother know? She doesn't exactly approve of me."

"She has no right to tell me who I can marry."

"Was that another proposal?" Krystal laughed. "I've told you before it'll take more than sweet words to win me over."

William sighed, leaning against the stone archway. "What can I do? How can I win the hand of the most beautiful girl in the village?"

Biting her lower lip, Krystal looked at the rose in her hands. "Gregory said if I married him, I'd never have to work a day in my life. He also said he'd buy me anything I wanted. My father approves of him—he doesn't approve of you—at least not yet. You would have to do something grand to win my hand, and my heart."

For the rest of the afternoon William tried to court Krystal, but she wouldn't be persuaded. Her will was as strong as his; she was determined to get her wish. With the sun nearing the treetops, William knew it was getting late, which meant his mother would be expecting him home any minute. "I have to go," he said. "Please don't accept Gregory's hand. Give me a chance to show your father that I'm a worthy suitor."

"Oh, here comes Gregory," said Krystal.

William followed her gaze in the direction of the sawmill. Gregory was strutting towards them—he looked like a Greek god. His sweaty, chiselled body was gleaming in the sunlight as William proceeded to leave. Nearing the edge of town, he glanced back to see Krystal admiring Gregory's physique. *The best-looking and wealthiest guy in town—how can I compete with that? I'll have to do something no one would expect,* William thought.

When he arrived home, William saw his mother sitting on the porch with Mary, enjoying some afternoon tea together. "How was work?" his mother asked.

"Tiring, like always," he replied.

"Really?" she said. "You don't look tired."

William shrugged his shoulders as he headed for the front door. "Aren't you going to say hello to Mary? She came by to pay us a visit."

William stopped for a moment. "Hello, Mary."

"Hello," she smiled, before he quickly went inside.

Later that night, William pondered his feelings. *My parents have always liked Mary, but they don't like Krystal. Mary's great, but she's nothing compared to Krystal. I know Krystal likes me, but I don't know if Mary does...*

His dilemma was quite serious, especially for a young man looking for a future spouse. Mary was shy and timid. She loved William dearly, but didn't know how to show it. She felt very threatened by Krystal, who many would say was more beautiful than Aphrodite herself. Mary could only hope that William would eventually look beyond Krystal's beauty, but *beauty* can be the most difficult illusion to break.

Chapter 2
A Grand Idea

The following morning, William thought about Krystal's words. Then he remembered where they were standing when she'd challenged him; the old stone archway in the centre of town. "The ancient path!" he gasped. According to legend, the old stone archway was said to be the place where a traveller would re-appear if they walked the ancient path and survived.

William sprung out of bed. He got dressed, quickly ate some breakfast, and kissed his mother goodbye. He went to Krystal's house and knocked on the door. It was early, but her father, the town clerk, was awake and soon opened it. "William?"

"I need to speak with you, Sir."

"Is this about Krystal?" he sighed.

"Um, sort of."

"Come in then," he said, holding the door open.

William stepped inside. The family wasn't wealthy, but he couldn't help but notice that their home was much nicer than his. "What's this all about?" her father asked, closing the door behind them.

"Is Krystal here?" William asked.

"Are you going to ask for her hand? I've already told you, my daughter will not be wed to a man whose pockets are empty."

"Your daughter challenged me to do something to win her hand," said William, "and I've come up with a grand idea."

"Well, what is it?" he asked.

"There's a path near the border of this town, a path from where none have returned."

"You're bloody daft!"

"I love your daughter, Sir, and if walking the ancient path will win her hand, then that's exactly what I'm prepared to do," William declared. "Is she here?"

"Yes, but she's still sleeping."

"Can you give her a message for me? Please tell her not accept Gregory until I return."

"I won't!" they heard a voice cry.

Krystal was indeed awake and had been listening to their conversation from the top of the staircase. As she came running down the stairs she jumped into William's arms. "You'd risk your life for my hand?! How romantic!" she said, kissing him on the cheek.

"I could be gone a while," said William.

"I know," she smiled. "But any man, who dares walk the ancient path and lives, would be the most famous man in the kingdom. I daresay his fame would bring much honour and wealth. Gregory has asked for my hand, but I haven't given him an answer. I'll wait for you, William. I'll be the envy of every girl in town!"

"You're already the envy of every girl in town," said her father.

"Oh, father!" she cried, stepping forward. "Surely, if William was to walk the ancient path and return, you would give your consent?"

With a deep sigh he turned to William, and said, "I have nothing against you, you know that. I just want what's best for Krystal. Gregory has the security that every father wants for his daughter. You come from a good family. Your father's a friend of mine, and I hope he returns soon. But what's going to happen if he doesn't? What if you walk the ancient path and never return? How do you think your mother will feel, having lost her husband and a son?"

"My father's a good fighter—it'd take more than a musket ball to stop him. My mother won't be losing either of us. I will survive the ancient path, because I'm driven by love, the most powerful thing of all," William replied.

"Have you ever walked the ancient path?"

"Well, I've walked about a hundred metres. Hasn't everyone?"

"Yes, but you haven't walked past the white tree, from where none have returned. It sits at the corner of a dark bend. Once you turn that corner, there's no coming back. Are you really prepared to risk your life for my daughter's hand? If it were up to me, I'd have you stay home and look after your mother."

William looked at Krystal's beautiful smile. "Yes, Sir, I certainly am. In fact, I'll leave tomorrow morning."

Krystal took William's hand. Looking deeply into his eyes, she softly kissed it, and said, "I'll be waiting for you. Hurry back to me."

"Alright," said her father. "Since I can't stop you, if you walk the ancient path and return by the magic gateway, you'll have my consent."

"Magic gateway?" said Krystal.

"Remember where we were yesterday? The old stone archway in the centre of town?" William reminded her. "That's where the ancient path ends, doesn't it, Sir?"

"Yes, according to legend."

"It doesn't matter. I'll find out soon enough," said William. "Anyway, I'd better be off, I'm working today."

Her father opened the door as Krystal walked him out. "I'm going to tell the whole town," she whispered. "You'll be famous before the day's gone."

William's hands began to feel cold and clammy. To appear brave, he straightened his back, puffed out his chest, then looked into the eyes of the town clerk, and said, "Thank you, Sir. I hope Krystal can see me off tomorrow?"

"I'd say the whole damn town'll be there," he chuckled. "Good luck," he said, shaking William's hand.

As her father was closing the door, Krystal blew William a kiss. *The whole town's gonna be there? What if I can't do it? I'll be the laughingstock of the kingdom,* he worried.

It was too late to take back his words. William had committed himself to a task, and come hell or high water—he had to accomplish it. With a sick feeling in the pit of his stomach, he headed off to work. By the end of the day, as he was heading home, the townsfolk were looking at him differently. Some pointed and whispered, some giggled softly, and others gave him a nod of respect.

The attention was too much, so he went home as quickly as he could. As he approached the house, he saw his mother and Mary sitting on the porch; they didn't look happy. "I guess you've heard?"

"Yes, we have!" said his mother.

"Can we not do this right now?" asked William, heading for the door.

"Oh, no you don't," she said, blocking his path. "Of all the women in this town, I'll not lose my son to a silly flirt, like Krystal!"

"She's not a flirt, Mother!"

"Of course she is," his mother replied, breathing heavily.

"I'm eighteen years old. I can make my own decisions, and if I want to marry Krystal, then I must do whatever it takes to win her hand."

"You're just like your father!" she cried. "I begged him not to leave for that stupid war, but now he's gone—I'll not lose my only son, too!"

"Father will return," said William. "You're not going to lose either of us. Now, may I please go inside? I have some packing to do."

Reluctantly, she stepped aside, allowing him to enter. As William was walking down the hallway, he heard his mother cry, "Don't do this! Is she really worth *dying* for?!"

Mary, who was sitting on the porch, could barely contain her grief; and when William's mother turned around… she was gone, having run away in tears.

Chapter 3

The Ancient Path

That night, William's mother spent hours trying to change his mind, but it was useless. Eventually, she had no choice but to concede, wishing him the best of luck. After all, she didn't want him leaving with bad blood between them.

The following morning William ate his breakfast, grabbed his blanket and pack, and headed out the door. Stepping off the porch, he noticed someone standing by the road. "Mary? Is that you? What are you doing out here in the cold?"

"I can't watch you go down that terrible path," she replied. "But I didn't want to miss you either, so I've been waiting since dawn."

William approached and wrapped his arms around her. "You're freezing! The door's unlocked if you want to go inside. I'm sure my mother will make you a nice cup of tea."

"Never mind," she said. "I have something important to say."

"Oh, okay, what is it?"

"Am I beautiful, William?" she asked.

William knew that Mary was beautiful. He didn't need to look her over, but proceeded to do so, only because she'd asked him. Mary's pale skin was white as pearl, her freckles were like tiny stars, and her long red hair was like fire. She was beautiful compared to most women, but average compared to Krystal. "Yes, you are. Why do you ask?"

"William, I've loved you since childhood," she cried. "I know you better than Krystal ever could. And I'm not the sort of woman who would see you risk your life just to win my hand. My hand has always been yours. You have only to ask for it."

For a brief moment William was captivated, then he remembered Krystal's beauty. "Look, I'm a bit confused," he choked. "But I'm still going to walk the ancient path."

"Before you leave, will you do something for me?"

"If it's within my power," William replied.

"Kiss me," said Mary. "I've waited my whole life for you to kiss me, and now I might never see you again. I'm not letting you go before you do."

As he looked into her eyes, William could feel a powerful force, like their souls had become intertwined. He began to kiss her, and what started out as something small quickly became long and passionate. By the time they had separated, William's feelings for Mary were stronger than ever. "Goodbye," she said, staring at him with a deep longing.

"B-bye…" he managed to utter.

Before he could say more a loud voice interrupted, "William!"

They turned to see one of the townsfolk. He was an older gentleman, who had worked with William's father at the Sawmill. "Lawrence?" said William. "What's wrong?"

"What are you doing standing around here?" he asked. "The whole town's waiting for you by the woods! Come!"

He gave him a nod, then smiled at Mary before walking away. Upon leaving her, William felt a pain in his heart. But when he saw the crowd gathered by the woods, he soon forgot about Mary as they began to cheer. Most were cheering, but some were mocking, doubting that he would make it past the legendary white tree.

The crowd parted as he approached; and, walking between them, he saw Krystal and her father waiting. They were standing by the tree-line, beside the ancient path. As he approached, Krystal walked up and kissed him on the cheek, causing the crowd to make a wooing sound. "Good luck," she said. "I know you'll come back to me."

William wanted to say something romantic but his thoughts turned to Mary. He was very confused, and just stood there with a smile on his face. Their moment was on the verge of becoming awkward. "Wait," said her father, breaking the silence, "we have a problem."

"A problem?" asked William.

"I hate to do this, but you'll have to leave your pack behind. According to tradition, you must walk the ancient path with nothing but the clothes on your back."

"Father!" Krystal protested.

"Those are the rules," he said, bluntly.

William sighed as he removed his pack, which had a blanket strapped to the back of it, and handed it to him. "Please make sure it gets back to my mother. Tell her not to worry."

"Of course."

"Go on, William! You can do it!" shouted a man in the crowd.

William smiled as they all erupted with cheers. He looked at Krystal, and said, "Wish me luck."

"Goodbye, my brave William," she replied. Unexpectedly, she kissed him on the lips, and said, "That's for luck."

With a cloud of bliss hanging over his head, William shook her father's hand before stepping onto the ancient path. As if a great force had silenced the crowd, barely a whisper could be heard. They watched as he went along, and when he reached the first corner, he made his way around the bend without looking back.

11

Cheers erupted again, but they soon fell silent, leaving William with nothing but his own thoughts. After a hundred metres, a sudden gust of wind kicked up, bringing to his nose a strong, earthy smell. Coloured leaves of red and gold danced across the path, rustling against the pebbles as they flew by. The sky was grey, yet moments ago it had been sunny. The rustling of the leaves and smell of the air was soothing to his senses. For the first time in his life, William felt completely alone, causing him to stop.

He thought about Mary's kiss. *No! I can't quit now. I'll be branded a coward for life.*

Reluctantly, he pushed on, looking for the infamous white tree. As he turned the next bend—he saw it. The path was straight for about a hundred yards, but it was unmistakeable. The tree was whiter than a spring lamb; its jagged branches leaned over the ancient path, like a clawed hand.

As he headed towards it, he felt an eerie sensation as he moved closer and closer. Standing before the white tree he noticed something peculiar. "Golden fruit?" he gasped. "I wonder what it tastes like."

The fruit of the tree was a shiny gold colour. It was circular in shape, and as he reached out and touched a small piece, William caught a glimpse of his own reflection in its golden skin. Then his eyes were drawn to the tree's beautiful leaves. They were whitish-silver, but were smooth to the touch, like silk. "This tree's not scary," he said to himself. "It's beautiful."

Removing a piece of the golden fruit, William held it close to his mouth, licking his lips as he prepared to bite. Suddenly, a shudder ran down his spine, as if death were fast approaching, causing him to drop it. As the fruit hit the ground, it split in half, spilling a dark, purple liquid. "Yuck!" he cried, jumping back.

The purple liquid seemed to bubble and boil as the fruit slowly disintegrated into nothing. The fruit of the tree meant certain death, and somehow, William knew it. With a chill in his bones he pressed on. When he turned the next bend he stopped again. "I went past the white tree," he realised. "No one in living memory who has passed the tree has ever returned."

Turning back, William looked around the corner for the white tree and almost collapsed in shock. The path was gone. Standing before him was a thick forest, full of long, spiny thorns. Any attempt to return the way he came would undoubtedly result in a slow and agonising death.

Chapter 4

Spiders and Frogs

With no way back, William was forced to continue along the ancient path.

For several kilometres he walked, and as he was heading past a great yew, a tiny figure jumped out in front of him. "Oh, no! They've sent another one!" the little man yelled, kicking up dirt and leaves with his tiny boots.

"Are you okay?" William asked.

"Me? I'm fine! It's you who's not okay! Oh, spiders and frogs!" he continued to cry, stomping about the path.

Observing the odd creature William realised he was a dwarf. Dwarves were known throughout the kingdom, but were seldom seen, especially in the vicinity of Geldirik. This particular dwarf, however, didn't appear to be well-off. His clothes and face were covered in dirt. His brown beard was full of leaves and twigs, and his curly black hair was just as messy. In short, he appeared to be a vagabond.

"Please, Sir," said William, "I'm afraid it's too late for me to turn back."

"Of course it is, stupid boy! You wouldn't be here if it weren't!"

William folded his arms and waited for the dwarf to calm down. After a moment or so, he finally ceased his stomping. "Are you going to tell me your name?" William asked. "You've been nothing but rude so far."

"That's it, boy! Put on a brave face!" said the dwarf. "But the smell of fear's all over you! Oh, spiders and frogs! Spiders and frogs!"

"Spiders and frogs?" William scoffed. "What does that mean?"

"They both eat flies, don't they? That's what you are, boy! You're nothing but a fly! Why they've sent you—I'll never know. Look at you! You're too young for a quest like this! They should've sent me another strong one. You'll not last the night, I expect!"

"My name's William. What's yours?"

Unexpectedly, the dwarf's demeanour changed to a polite tone. "Oh, I do apologise. My name's Noble—I'll be your guide," he said, shaking William's hand.

"My guide to what?"

"Where do you think you are?!" the dwarf yelled, his demeanour changing again. "You're standing on the path of sin, boy! Those who fail to conquer it—die in it! Seven times you'll be tested. Many have tried. Some were looking for glory and honour. Others came for wealth and prosperity, but what brings you here? You don't look like much."

"I took this quest to win the hand of the fairest maiden in town."

The dwarf removed a twig from his long, scraggly beard. "You're doing it for love?"

William hesitated. "Yes, that's right. I'm doing it for love."

"You sound confused…"

"Look, I don't think it matters why I'm doing this," said William. "I have my reasons, okay? Now, are you going to be my guide or what?"

The dwarf chuckled. "Very well, but I'll not be responsible for your safety. I'm a guide—that's it. I can't slay any demons for you, got it?"

"Okay," William agreed.

After following him for some time, the silence was almost deafening. "Did you say I'd be tested seven times?" William asked.

"That's right," Noble replied.

"What about the white tree? Was that a test?"

"Ha!" the dwarf cackled. "That was just a warm-up! Not everything you encounter on the ancient path will be a test. Some things are lessons to be learned, others are simply there, but nothing's without purpose, and nothing's ever the same. The path knows who's walking it. It knows your every sin, and it knows your every fault and fear, understand?"

"I think so, Noble? Was that your name?"

"Yes, boy, you may call me that."

After travelling a bit further, William saw something up ahead. There appeared to be two figures, sitting by the trees, to the left of the path. "Look," he gasped. "What are they doing here? Is this my first test?"

"I cannot say," Noble replied. "That would be breaking the rules."

They quietly approached and were soon standing behind them. Strangely, William knew they weren't human. They looked human enough; both were men, but one was very old and the other was young. Stranger still, they were both painting landscapes. They were sitting in wooden chairs, quite separate from each other, with a brush in one hand and a palette in the other. "Hello," said William.

They both ignored him. William moved closer and looked over the young painter's shoulder. He had golden blonde hair, fair skin, and was wearing a white shirt and pants. He had a peaceful smile on his face and was humming a low tune as he continued to paint his masterpiece, and what a masterpiece it was. "Oh, wow! That looks amazing—it's so incredibly detailed!" William remarked, but the young man refused to acknowledge him.

Stepping around, William examined it more closely. It was a painting of a beautiful, golden country, filled with green pastures, animals, and exotic flowers. William looked directly into his eyes, but still the young man didn't react. Then he heard the sound of weeping. He glanced over at the old man and saw him covering his face with his hands, crying like a child. William looked at Noble; the dwarf shrugged his shoulders. Approaching the old man, William softly touched his shoulder. "Are you okay, Sir?"

The old man stopped and looked up, but not at William. "Why won't it work? Why doesn't it ever work?" he cried, staring at his painting.

William looked at it and almost gagged. It was the most hideous thing he had ever seen. It was another landscape, but everything was terribly distorted. Looking at the old man's face, he noticed it was covered in specks and stripes of paint. His complexion was pale, with a green tinge, and his clothes were ragged and worn; he looked sickly, and his wrinkles were deep and full of memory. "Please don't cry," he said, but the old man ignored him.

Bewildered, William approached Noble, who didn't seem concerned. "What is this? I can't make any sense of it…"

"They're the painters of life," he replied. "One has painted a good life for himself, the other has not."

"Why can't the old man paint a good one?" asked William.

"Because he's missing something, and he's made many bad decisions."

"What is he missing?"

"I can't tell you," said Noble, "but one day you'll understand."

Chapter 5

The Angel of Death

William wanted to help the old man but the painters still refused to acknowledge him, and so they continued along the ancient path.

The woods on both sides began to slowly change, but the path itself remained the same. It didn't get wider or narrower, and the pebbles continued to crunch beneath their feet. They had been silent for a while, but just when William was about to open his mouth, he noticed a dark figure coming towards them—it was a knight.

"Is this a test?" William asked.

"I told you I can't answer that!" Noble barked.

The knight was riding aggressively and sporadically. His entire body covered in dark armour. William began to fear he would have to dive off the path, but the armoured figure pulled the reins of his huge black horse, bringing the intimidating creature to a halt, albeit uncomfortably close to where he stood. William could feel it's breath on his face and smell the metallic odour of what looked like blood oozing from its mouth. "G-g-good afternoon, Sir," he stammered.

As the knight removed something from a small bag attached to his saddle, William could've sworn he heard him hiss like a serpent. With something golden in his hand, the knight moved closer. Holding out his arm, he opened his black glove to reveal a piece of golden fruit. It was the fruit of the white tree. "I-I'm sorry," William choked, "but I must decline your gift. I'm not feeling well, you see."

The knight dropped the fruit. William's first instinct was to retrieve it, but something stopped him from doing so. Suddenly, the knight's visor flew open, causing William to jump back in terror. Beneath the knight's armour was a skeleton of charred bones, with bright purple eyes. They flashed like fire, burning into his soul. Opening his mouth, the skeleton began to cackle. It was the most evil laugh William had ever heard. And just when he was about to turn and run, the knight's horse violently reared up, before charging down the ancient path.

"What the hell was that?!" William cried, shaking with adrenaline.

"That was the Angel of Death," Noble replied, bluntly.

"Weren't you afraid?"

"Why should I be afraid? He can't hurt me. I'm the guide of the ancient path, remember?"

William stared at him, struggling to comprehend the dwarf's nature. So far, William had seen some strange things, but he never expected to encounter such horror. "Well, was that a test or not?"

"I can't tell you what *is* or *isn't* a test. But I'll tell you when you've passed one."

"What happens if I don't pass?"

"Then you'll most likely be dead."

"Oh, that's comforting," said William, rolling his eyes.

After walking along the path for a few more hours, the sun was starting to set. "I think we'll bed down for the night," said Noble.

"In the middle of the path?" William questioned. "What if the Angel of Death returns? Why don't we camp in the woods?"

"Nothing will harm you as long as you don't stray too far from the path. Besides, the woods are dangerous at night. Gather some wood, and I'll make a fire."

William nodded his head, and stepped into the woods. "But remember," said Noble, "don't stray too far."

After gathering some wood, William set it down in the middle of the path. Glancing at the horizon, the sun was almost down; the air was getting colder by the minute. "Please, Noble," said William, "please start the fire—I'm freezing."

"Why didn't you bring a blanket?" he asked.

"The town clerk said it was tradition to walk the ancient path with nothing but the clothes on your back."

"Ha!" Noble laughed. "Shows you how much he knows! Many knights have travelled this path with mighty steeds, laden with provisions. For some, the journey is long and cumbersome, taking many months. But for others, the journey may only take a few days."

"How can that be?" said William. "What exactly is the ancient path?"

"I've already told you it's the path of sin. It exists between life and death; if you reach the end, then one you will find. The path knows you—it will tempt you at every turn."

William watched as Noble leaned forward and spat on the pile of wood, causing it to suddenly come alight. "Hey, how'd you do that?"

"The guide of the ancient path can do as he wishes… within reason."

William rubbed his hands together and held them close to the fire. "I wish we had some food. Can you make food appear?"

"I could," Noble replied, "but it wouldn't be fair."

William wasn't sure what the dwarf meant but decided to change the subject. "Is it really true that no one's ever made it to the end?"

"Only one has."

"Really? What's his name? Where is he?"

"He's everywhere," said Noble, looking up at the stars. "You can't meet him face to face in your world, but you'll meet him in the next."

"The next?"

"When you're dead."

"That doesn't sound good," William sighed.

"Hahaha!" the dwarf chuckled.

"What?" said William. "What's so funny about that?"

"The way you humans speak of death, as if it's something you can avoid. It always makes me laugh."

"Aren't you afraid of dying?" William asked.

"We all owe God a death, so why should I fear that which is inevitable?"

William couldn't think of a worthy rebuttal. Several hours passed. He tried to sleep, but the ground was uncomfortable; and to make matters worse, he could hear Noble snoring away, which only increased his frustration. Eventually, he managed to drift off for a while, but was soon awoken by the sounds of laughter.

Chapter 6

The Faeries of Folly

At first, William thought it was his imagination, caused by lack of sleep. But as the laughter grew louder, he reluctantly sat up.

The fire was getting dim. He placed more wood onto it; and as the flames began to rise, he caught a glimpse of eye-shine. Startled, William stood up and peered into the surrounding forest. A figure stepped out from behind a tree. He couldn't tell what it was, but its eyes were glowing green in the firelight. He glanced at Noble; the dwarf was still snoring away, with his head resting on a log.

To his surprise, when he looked at the forest again, he saw more eyes peering back at him through the darkness. He slowly turned in a circle; they were everywhere. Every now and then, he heard another giggle of laughter. Suddenly, something ran straight past him. It was ever so quick, and its wild laughter was finally enough to wake Noble.

"Grrr… spiders and frogs!" he coughed. "What's going on?"

"Shhh!" said William. "There're creatures all around us."

Noble looked about as laughter echoed throughout the forest. "Oh, it's the night of faeries—this is a night of folly for them. I'd stay close to the fire if I were you."

"Are they dangerous?"

"Not really," he yawned, and closed his eyes.

"You're going back to sleep?"

"Yes, and I suggest you do the same," he snorted.

William was tired, but too curious and fearful to sleep. The sounds stopped for a while, so he tended the fire a bit more. However, the laughter soon returned. Glancing up, he peered into the darkness.

"Psst!" he heard someone say.

William watched in disbelief as a female figure with glowing green eyes stepped out of the woods. "Are you a faerie?"

"Don't wake Noble," she said, stepping into the light of the fire.

William's eyes widened. Standing before him was a strange-looking woman, with pale green skin, long purple hair, and green, luminous eyes. "Are you wearing leaves?" he asked, swallowing hard. "How are you acquainted with Noble?"

"Leaves are a faerie's clothes," she giggled. "As for Noble, well, he used to be a lot of fun, but not anymore—not since he became a guide. But you, William, you're not a guide. Will you come and play with us?"

"Us?" he asked, nervously.

Tilting her head towards the woods, the faerie smiled back at him. Reluctantly, William looked into the black trees and saw several pairs of glowing, green eyes. For a brief moment he felt like yelling to alert Noble, but he didn't want to be seen as a coward, especially if they were just playing a trick. William stood up and took a few steps towards the woods. "What kind of games do you play?"

The faeries moved closer, with some approaching from behind, surrounding him and cutting off any chance of escape. Reaching out, they began to stroke his bare skin. "W-what are you doing?" he asked.

"What does it feel like we're doing?" said the purple-haired faerie, pushing her body up against him. "Come into the woods and play, where many pleasures await you."

"I can't," he replied. "I have to stay on the path."

"We won't take you far," said the faerie, before kissing him on the lips.

Her scent was intoxicating, like some rare and exotic flower. Before he could reply, the faeries were pulling him away from the path. Stepping into the woods, he saw dozens of them, dancing provocatively, making strange gestures towards him. They gathered around, but then William's thoughts turned to Krystal and Mary. "No!" he cried, pulling himself away.

"Quick! Grab him!" one of the faeries hissed, as William ran back to the safety of the ancient path as swiftly as he could.

"Thank God," he said, reaching the fire, where Noble was still snoring away. Glancing back, he saw their glowing eyes in the distance, but they now seemed reluctant to approach. "That was scary," he whispered to himself. "My father was right."

All throughout the night, William tended the fire, keeping an eye out for faeries. Every now and then, he would hear a soft giggle, but by morning the sounds were gone. "Wake up!" said Noble, kicking his leg.

"Ouch!" William cried. "What was that for?"

"That was for leaving the path last night!"

"How'd you know?"

"There's a difference between pretending to be asleep and actually sleeping."

"Oh," he said, standing up. "Then why didn't you stop me?"

"Because you were being tested," Noble replied.

"I failed, didn't I?"

A tiny smiled formed in the corners of his mouth. "No, my boy, you passed!"

"I passed? But I left the path…"

"Yes, but you resisted temptation. Most men your age wouldn't have been able to resist a faerie's touch. What made you come back?"

"I thought about Krystal and Mary. I also remembered something my father said to me, long ago. He wasn't a man of honour in his youth. That is, until he met my mother."

"What did he tell you?" asked Noble.

"He said the action of a moment can cause a lifetime of regret."

"Right he would be! Believe me; you'd be dead by now if you'd been led astray by lust. But you're still alive, and you've passed the first test."

William took a deep breath. "Okay. What's next?"

"I can't tell you!" the dwarf growled. "And you should know better than to ask!"

"Okay, okay, I'm sorry!"

"Come, boy. We've got a long day ahead of us."

With a great yawn, William stretched out his arms. "I sure am hungry. Is there any food nearby?"

"Perhaps," Noble replied, as he continued to walk away.

"Wait! Shouldn't we put out the fire?"

Noble turned around with a sigh. "How long's it going to take you to learn? This path is magic. Now, let the fire be. It'll go out in its own time."

They continued along the ancient path. There was a light mist in the air, but not a hint of wind. But as the sun began to rise a bit higher the mist became clearer, allowing them to see the path ahead. Many kilometres they walked, with William's thirst and hunger increasing each step of the way. "What's that growling noise?" asked Noble.

"It's my stomach," William replied.

"Why's it doing that?"

William stopped and stared at him. "Because I'm hungry. Haven't you ever experienced hunger pains?"

"Not that I recall. But I can smell food up ahead."

"Really?" he smiled. "You better not be messing with me."

"Come! Let's see what's around the next bend."

Chapter 7

Sweet as Honey

As they were turning the next bend William could hear voices. He could also detect the smell of food, and as the path straightened up, they came upon an extraordinary sight.

Sitting in the middle of the path was a great banquet. There was a large table of oak, surrounded by four chairs, two of which were already occupied. However, they weren't occupied by people, they were occupied by animals.

"What the—" said William, unable to finish his sentence.

"What's wrong?" asked Noble. "Haven't you ever seen a fox and a pig having lunch together?"

William couldn't take his eyes off the strange characters. They were definitely animals, but they were also humanoid. They had arms and legs, were quite tall, and were sitting up like humans. Not only that—they were also wearing clothes. "Oi, look 'ere! We've got company!" said the pig.

"Oh, how delightful," the fox exclaimed. "Won't you join us, friends?"

William stared at Noble. "Don't look at me. I'm not hungry."

"Am I allowed to?"

"You have free will, don't you?" said Noble, folding his arms.

"Forget your cranky friend!" the pig snorted. "Come join us! There's plenty for all!"

William slowly approached the table and sat down. Despite the glorious banquet of assortments in front of him, he couldn't take his eyes off the animals. "Hello, young man," said the fox. "Allow me to introduce myself: my name is Cyril, and my companion is Truffles."

"Oh, put a bloody sock in it!" said the pig. "Can't you see the boy's 'ungry?!"

"Come now, Truffles, it's polite to greet a guest."

"Not when the food's gettin' cold!" the pig snorted.

"Um, my name's William."

"Nice to meet you, William," Cyril replied. "Please, help yourself to any food you like, but try not to take anything in front of Truffles. He can be rather protective of his food; and if you would like me to pass you anything, please don't hesitate to ask. It's quite rude to reach across a table you know."

William sat and watched as the pig scoffed down a few pieces of pie, some cupcakes, and a plate of roast beef. His face was now covered with food, and his grey shirt was filthy. William looked at the fox. He was neatly dressed, was wearing a green suit, and his red fur was nicely combed. "What's with you? Aren't you goin' to eat somethin'?" asked Truffles.

Nodding his head, William surveyed the banquet. In front of him were a few pieces of bread, some grapes, and a pitcher of red wine. "Oh, drat," said Cyril, before tossing his plate of food on the ground, causing it to break into several pieces.

"What's wrong?" asked William, as Truffles began to laugh.

"Oh, it just wasn't right," Cyril replied. "I didn't cut the chicken well enough—they should have been even squares. I cut the carrots too thick, the pudding was too dry, and the plate had a scratch on it."

William glanced back at Noble. He was leaning against a nearby tree, ignoring them. Looking at the food in front of him, William's stomach continued to rumble. He took a few pieces of bread and some grapes, and put them on his plate. "Excuse me," said Cyril, "but may I make a suggestion?"

"Sure," he replied.

"Your plate looks nice, but it needs a little more colour. You might want to add some green or something—that'll do the trick."

"Who cares how it looks, as long as it tastes good!" said Truffles, before stuffing his face with another piece of pie.

William felt sick upon seeing the mess that Truffles was making, yet he couldn't help but agree with the pig. He didn't see any point in trying to make his meal look decorative. So, refusing the fox's advice, William ate some bread and grapes, then drank some red wine. The food was exquisite; he could imagine himself spending the whole day at the table, but he still had a quest to complete. He was tempted to try some of the sweet cakes, but decided not to; and after having a few glasses of water, he stood up to leave. "Oi! Where're you goin'?" said Truffles. "You ain't finished already? Don't you wanna try some of these cakes? They're sweet'er than honey!"

"No thanks," he replied. "I have a long journey ahead of me."

"Then why not take something with you?" Cyril suggested.

"Yeah," said Truffles. "You could put somethin' in your pockets."

"Don't be absurd," Cyril growled. "He can take one of our plates."

"How? You've already smashed most of 'em!" Truffles chuckled.

"Guys!" said William, loudly. "It's okay. I don't need anything more. I thank you for the meal, and for your kindness, but I must be off."

"It's very rude to leave without dessert," said Cyril.

"What about your scruffy-lookin' friend? He hasn't eaten yet," said Truffles.

William left the table and approached Noble. "Can we go, please?"

"Yes, we can," he replied, leading the way.

They headed around the table as Truffles continued to stuff his face, and as they were walking away, William heard the sound of Cyril smashing another plate on the ground. "That was the weirdest thing I've ever seen."

"You should be jumping up and down with joy."

"Why?" he asked.

"Because you've just passed your second test," Noble revealed.

"That was a test?"

"Indeed it was! And this time you passed with flying colours."

"Okay, but how was that a test? I just ate some bread and grapes?"

"You drank some wine, too, didn't you?"

"Well, yeah, and a few glasses of water. There wasn't anything poisonous on that table, was there?" he worried.

"Of course not," Noble laughed. "But you did the right thing: you didn't eat too much, and you weren't fussy about it either."

"Okay, but I still don't see how that could've been a test."

"One day you'll understand."

Further and further they walked, then William stopped dead in his tracks. Something was coming towards them. "What is it?" asked Noble.

"There's a rider in the distance," William replied, with a slight quiver in his voice.

"So?"

"Don't you remember the Angel of Death? What if it's him again?"

"Ridiculous!" Noble replied. "That's not the Angel of Death. It's the white knight, and he happens to be a friend of mine. He won't harm you."

"I thought you couldn't tell me these things?"

"Yes, but the white knight isn't from the ancient path—he's from another place. Though, I don't know what he's doing here."

As they got closer, the white knight picked up speed. He was now tearing towards them; William stepped to the side, preparing to dive into the woods. But as the knight was almost upon them, he stopped abruptly, and jumped off his horse. He was dressed in beautiful, shining armour, with a white feather atop his helm. As he approached, he appeared to be removing his sword-belt. "Here you go, lad!" he yelled. "You're going to need this," he said, handing his sword to William.

"Hi, my name's William," he replied.

"I know," said the knight, removing his armour.

"Um… what are you doing?"

"I told you, lad, you'll need these more than I. The horse is yours, too."

William stared at him in bewilderment. "Please, Sir Knight, I could never take your horse and armour. I'm just a lowly peasant—a mill-worker."

"Don't say that!" the knight snapped. "You're more than you realise."

William looked at Noble, who didn't seem surprised by the knight's actions. And, before he knew it, the knight was walking away in nothing but his breeches. "Wait!" he cried. "Please, Sir Knight! You must tell me your name!"

The knight glanced back. "My name is Gabriel."

Before William could respond, Gabriel stepped into the forest and vanished. "Well, what are you waiting for?" said Noble. "Put the armour on!"

Chapter 8

Dragon's Hoard

With Noble's instruction, William put the armour on and tied the sword-belt around his waist. Then he approached the white horse; it was a magnificent stallion, and attached to the back of the saddle, was a bag of provisions.

William sifted through it. There was plenty of bread and fruit, plus a cask of wine and some water. "I can't believe he gave me all this."

"The owner of the path sent him, which means you've gained favour in his eyes. Perhaps I was too quick to judge," said Noble.

"You didn't think I'd get this far, did you?" he asked, looking at the silver shield hanging from the saddle.

"No," the dwarf admitted. "I thought you were too young for such a quest."

"I guess age doesn't matter."

"True, but in most cases—it does."

"What's this mean?" asked William, admiring the four-pointed star on the shield. "The shield's coated with silver, but I think the star's made of gold."

"That's the morning star," said Noble. "And yes, it is made of gold."

William mounted the white horse. "There's still enough room if you want to ride with me?" he said, looking down at the dwarf.

"No," he chuckled. "Don't worry; if you ride slowly, I'll be able to keep up."

They continued along the ancient path, with William riding tall on his new horse. The sky soon became dark, but it did not rain. There was no wind either, making the next part of their journey rather eerie. Noble suddenly stopped. "What is it?" said William.

"You must go inside," the dwarf replied, pointing towards a large cave.

It was located about ten yards inside the forest. "Wait, is this a test? You said I couldn't leave the path?"

"You can in this instance. I can't tell you if it's a test, but I can tell you what's inside?"

"Okay. What's in there?"

"A cruel and vile creature," Noble revealed. "I can't tell you what to do, but know this: the dragon within has killed many innocent people and plundered their wealth."

"Dragon?" William gasped. "Does it breathe fire? How big is it?"

"I can tell you no more…"

William dismounted his horse and removed the shield hanging from the saddle. Leaving the path, he took a few steps into the forest, then glanced back. "It's so dark inside. How will I see with this helmet on?"

"Never mind," said Noble. "There'll be plenty of light inside."

William shook his head; he could scarcely believe he was about to face a dragon. The mouth of the cave was large, and he couldn't see a glimmer of light as he went inside. Fearing he was about to be attacked, he drew his sword. He stopped for a moment and listened. He could hear water dripping from the ceiling, but there was something else; it was a low hissing or breathing sound. Then he realised it was the dragon's breath.

Heading deeper into the cave, the walls began to close around him. The walled path ahead was covered in sharp, jagged rocks. He tried to step quietly, but each time he bumped into the walls, his armour would make a clanging sound. He raised the visor on his helmet. The stale air was putrid with the smell of decay. Unexpectedly, the path ended, and the cave opened up into a great hollow. "I see light," he whispered to himself.

Moving forward, the cave was becoming brighter. Small fires were everywhere; they seemed to be dancing on pools of water. The walls of the cave were glowing with bits of red and orange, and as William reached an incline, he glanced down to see a pile of sparkling yellow. "Gold!" he gasped.

At the bottom of the rocky hill was a great hoard. He could see thousands of gold coins, precious jewels, an assortment of vessels, and old statues. The breathing sound was loud, then he noticed something red—it was the dragon. It was nestled in the middle of the hoard, seemingly asleep.

"That's it?" he said. The beast was no bigger than a horse. The dragon was small, but its tail and neck were long, and its jagged teeth were like that of a crocodile. Its bright red scales shimmered and glowed in the light of the fires, and its small wings flapped, ever so slightly, in tune with its breath.

Slowly, William made his way down the hill. Suddenly, he slipped on the wet rocks. Falling forward, he desperately struggled to regain his footing, but it was too late. Some of the loose rocks fell towards the pile of gold, bouncing and crashing as they went. "Who's there?" said the dragon, opening its eyes.

William quickly pulled down his visor and froze as the beast looked up. "Is that you, Gabriel? Is my time here finished? Has the day of the Lord finally arrived?"

"No," said William, slowly raising his visor again. "It is I, William, of Geldirik."

"I see," said the dragon. "My name is Seraphace. How I have longed for Gabriel's shield of silver and gold. Care to make a trade?"

"No," William replied. "But I do have a bargain for you."

"Oooo! Sounds exciting!" the dragon hissed. "Pray, tell me, what is this bargain?"

"I have a friend waiting outside, and he told me that you've killed many innocents and stolen their wealth. Is it true?"

"Of course! Gold is what I covet most. I don't care who has it, or where it comes from—it's going to be mine."

"Even at the cost of your own life?"

"What is your meaning, boy?!" the dragon snarled, as it rose to its feet.

"You deserve death for what you've done!" said William, raising his sword and shield.

The dragon lowered its head. "You're right, I do deserve death, but what's done is done. How about this: spare my life and I'll give you half my plunder."

William lowered his sword, staring at the glistening hoard. "That's it, boy! I see the greed in your eyes! Imagine what you could buy for your family. You could live a life of ease and comfort. You could be waited-on by others for the rest of your life. You'll never have to work your fingers to the bone again. What say you?"

After a brief moment of contemplation, William slammed down his visor, raised his sword, and charged towards the beast. "Aaargh!" Seraphace cried, jumping back.

He tried to flee, but the gold beneath his clawed feet was making him slip. When he realised that William was almost upon him, Seraphace roared, breathing a shower of fire. It flew and spun through the air towards him. William dropped to one knee and held up his shield as the flames struck.

Safely behind it, he could see flames to his left and right. When the flames stopped, William jumped through a haze of smoke and smote the dragon on its head with his sword. "Aaargh!" Seraphace cried, falling on his back.

Without hesitation, William drove his sword into the chest of the beast, then swung at its neck, cutting off its head. Struggling to breathe, William was forced to remove his helmet. He took a few deep breaths as he watched the dragon's body flinch and kick. A moment later, he breathed a sigh of relief. Its body was now lifeless as its severed head.

Suddenly, he heard a hissing sound. Believing the dragon had come back to life, William got such a fright that he dropped his helmet, which rolled across some gold coins before sinking into one of the fiery pools of water. Then he realised the dragon's body was dissolving into a slimy, purple liquid. "It's just like the golden fruit," he gasped.

"Well done!" he heard a voice shout.

Turning around, he saw Noble standing at the top of the rocky hill. Without saying a word, William made his way up the incline. "What are you doing? Are you crazy, boy?" said Noble. "Are you just going to leave the gold where it is?"

Reaching the top, William stared at him with sadness in his eyes. "You've just slain the beast!" the dwarf cried. "And you won't even take a single coin?"

"I don't see any gold down there," said William, solemnly. "All I see is blood."

Noble smiled. "Then, what's to be done with it?"

"Give it to the families of the dragon's victims," he said, before walking away.

Noble stared at the great hoard for a moment, then followed him out of the cave. "Congratulations, boy, you've passed your third test!"

"Figured as much," he replied.

"What's the matter, boy?"

"That's what's the matter!" William barked. "For almost two days I've been travelling with you, and you're still calling me *boy!* My name is *William!*"

"Oh, spiders and frogs!" said Noble, waving his arms about. "Alright… William it is. It's not easy for me, you know! I've been guiding young men for God knows how long. And all of them have failed. Getting attached to those I guide can be quite painful, understand?"

"Yes, I think I do."

After giving his sword and shield a quick clean, William mounted his horse. "You said that one had reached the end of the ancient path? You said he was everywhere. Who was he? Was he Gabriel?"

"No," said Noble, "but Gabriel serves him. Now, no more questions. We still have a long day ahead of us."

Chapter 9

The Immovable Object

For another hour they travelled, then stopped for a quick lunch. Once again, Noble refused to eat, as if he were invulnerable to hunger and thirst. William tried to feed his new horse, but the beast refused to eat or drink as well—it was very odd.

The dark clouds rolled away as they continued their journey. The midday sun was now high in the sky. As they were turning the next corner, they came upon a bridge. It was a long, wooden one, stationed over a deep chasm. They were about to cross, but something was blocking the way. "Is that what I think it is?" asked William, staring at the massive object.

"Yes," said Noble, "it's a big, fat dragon."

"Not another one!"

"I'm afraid so."

Slowly and cautiously they approached the bridge. As the dragon raised its head, they both stopped. "Excuse me," said William, "but we need to cross."

"What's your rush?" the dragon smiled. "Why not take a rest?"

"I'm on a very important quest," said William. "Can you please get off the bridge, so we can pass? It's not right to rest in such a place."

"Oh, but I'm tired," the dragon moaned. "Just let me rest for a few more minutes. You can rest with me, if you like?"

Just then, a great rumbling sound came from the beast, followed by a terrible stench. "Aaargh!" Noble cried, holding his nose. "What've you been eating? Don't you know it's rude to pass wind in front of others?"

"Ha!" the dragon laughed. "Why should I care? I do what I like. No one tells me when to move. I was here first, so you'll just have to go around."

"Go around?!" William spluttered, staring at the endless chasm. "That could take days! We're not going around just because you're too lazy to move. Get up! Let us pass or I'll have no choice but to slay you where you sit!"

"Very well," the dragon sighed. "I'll move, but only if you let me rest for five more minutes?"

William glanced at Noble. "What should I do?"

"Don't look at me—I'm just a guide."

"Alright, dragon," he replied. "You can rest for five more minutes, but that's all."

The beast yawned, then let out a high-pitched whistle. William and Noble watched as a bird appeared in the sky with a cluster of berries. The dragon opened its mouth. They continued to watch with fascination as the bird dropped the berries into its gaping jaws before flying away. "That's how you get your food?" William asked. "When was the last time you actually moved?"

"You mean… off the bridge?"

"Yeah."

"Why should I move? The birds bring me food and water, and there's a nice gap between these planks beneath me," the dragon chuckled.

"A gap between the—" said William, furrowing his brow before his expression suddenly turned sour. "That's gross!"

"Each to their own," the dragon yawned, closing its eyes.

They waited for five minutes. The beast remained motionless. Then William dismounted and drew his sword. "Okay, dragon, your five minutes are up! Time to move!"

"Already? But I'm still tired!" the beast complained. "Just give me a couple of hours. Then I'll move—I promise."

"No!" William cried. "Absolutely not! Get off this bridge right now, or I'll have no choice but to kill you! What's it gonna be?"

"But it's only a couple of hours," the beast yawned.

"That's it! I've had enough!" said William, marching forward.

The dragon looked at him. He knew the boy was armed, but even the threat of death could not convince him to budge. The dragon's body was so large that William was forced to climb upon him. With his sword aimed at the dragon's head, he yelled, "Okay! This is your last chance! Are you going to move or not?!"

The dragon looked up at him. "This is *my* spot! Go get your own!"

"If this's your resting place, then let it be so—permanently!" William cried, before bringing his blade down upon the dragon's head, landing a killing blow. Suddenly, he began to hear a hissing sound. "Uh, oh!" he cried, leaping off its body.

Once he was off the bridge, William looked back to see the dragon's carcass slowly turn into that same purple liquid as before. It spewed and bubbled as it slid off the bridge, oozing between the wooden planks. "What is that stuff?"

With the bridge clear Noble smiled at him. "Well done, William! You've passed the fourth test—only three more to go!"

"Thanks," he replied.

"No need to thank me. I didn't slay the dragon."

"Thanks for calling me by my name."

"Oh," the dwarf chuckled. "Of course you did."

"You call that a test?" said William, shaking his head. "It doesn't make any sense. Why wouldn't he just move? All he had to do was move and he'd still be alive."

"One day you'll understand," the dwarf replied, before heading across the bridge.

Not wishing the hooves of his steed to get caught between the planks, William took the reins and led his horse across the bridge. The bridge creaked and groaned. Reaching the other side, barely a tree had a brown leaf, and the ground was chilled with frost. "I wasn't expecting this," said William.

"You're halfway now," said Noble. "Things will be different on this side of the forest, but don't be discouraged."

Mounting his horse, they continued along the ancient path; William could feel the icy air blowing off the frosty ground, yet his horse didn't mind at all. After a while, the wind dropped and the trees ceased their creaking, leaving them surrounded by a dead silence. All they could hear were the sounds of their feet stepping on the frozen leaves.

They had been travelling almost an hour, when a sudden sound caused William's horse to rear up with fright. "Easy," he said, stroking the beast's neck. There was a sinister laugh in the air, but William couldn't discern the direction. "What was that?"

The dwarf stopped in his tracks. "It's your next test," he said. "And this one's different from the others."

"I thought you couldn't tell me when it's a test?"

"Normally I can't," said Noble. "I can't tell you what to do. But I can tell you what not to do, if you like?"

"That'd be nice for a change," William replied.

"Around the next bend you'll see a strange creature," Noble began to say, "and no matter what he says or does, you mustn't respond. Do not allow yourself to be baited by his pranks. Is that clear?"

"Okay."

Just like Noble said, when they turned the next corner, William caught sight of a figure standing on the path. At first, he thought it was a man. Its upper half was human enough, but its ears were pointed; and on its head, were two curved ram's horns, and from the waist down, it had the legs and cloven hooves of a goat. It was definitely a faun.

"A little man, and a big man, dressed like a kettle drum!" the faun laughed. "That armour doesn't fit you properly, foolish boy! I bet you're not even a real knight!"

William looked at Noble, who remained silent, barely acknowledging the faun's presence, except for a glance. As if he could fly, the faun suddenly leapt into the forest and disappeared. "Is that it? Is it over?" William asked.

Expecting a quick reply, Noble refused to respond. The dwarf didn't even look at him. "Noble? Why are you ignoring me?"

"Look!" they heard a voice shout. "It's a stupid little boy, pretending to be a knight! What an embarrassment to his family he must be!"

William recognised the faun's voice but couldn't see him anywhere. He was trailing them from the confines of the forest, and for the next half hour his abuse continued. There were moments of silence, but the faun's teasing was intolerable. And to make matters worse, William had no support from Noble. The dwarf was silent as the grave.

They pressed on, but the faun wouldn't stop. After an hour had passed, the faun took his abuse to another level. William had remained silent, refusing to react, but as they were turning another corner, he was struck in the chest by a rock. "Ahahaha!" the faun cackled. "You even sound like a kettle drum!"

William's face was red; he squeezed the reins as hard as he could. For the next few hours, he continued to take the faun's abuse. He copped the occasional stone's throw, which was more frustrating to deal with. For the rest of the day he showed great restraint, and as the twilight hour approached—the faun vanished.

When Noble finally stopped and smiled at him, William burst into tears. "I know, son," said the dwarf, solemnly. "But you've passed the fifth test."

"I've never wanted to kill something so badly in all my life!" he sobbed and sniffled. "The worst part was your silence!"

"I know, son, but it's over now."

Chapter 10

The Magic Mirror

They made camp for the night. William was haunted by the faun's words. Never in his life had words affected him so; it made him think about his own words, and the terrible things he had said to others.

Sitting by the firelight, Noble was concerned by his silence. "Are you okay? I hope you didn't take his words to heart?"

"I know I'm not a real knight," he replied. "But I wish I was…"

"Every man does at some point."

"Should I be wearing this armour?"

"It was a gift, wasn't it?" said Noble. "Gabriel would not have relinquished his armour if he thought you unworthy of it. Take comfort in that. If this lesson has taught you anything, it's the power of words. Words can be used for good or evil. The faun could've used his words to uplift you, but his intent was to break you."

William took a deep breath. "When I was younger, there was this strange-looking boy who used to live in Geldirik; all the kids used to tease him. Sometimes I joined-in… but now I wish I hadn't."

"Good," said Noble. "Words are a powerful thing. The very universe, in which we live, was spoken into existence by the words of God. Never forget how powerful they are, and always think before you speak."

It was the morning of the third day. The night had been cold, but they'd kept the fire up, which helped somewhat. William was tired. The supplies Gabriel had given him were running low. Yet, Noble still hadn't eaten a thing; it was the same for William's horse.

There was no wind, and the icy morning was chilly as they turned the next bend. To William's surprise, they came upon a land of snow. The path was powdered white; the trees were frozen stiff, with icicles hanging from every branch. "What's this?" he said, shivering. "It's not supposed to snow for another month."

"Like many other worlds, the ancient path exists between life and death," said Noble. "Only once have I seen snow on this path… and it was just before the end."

"I've got two more tests to complete, don't I?"

"Yes, but the path of sin doesn't belong to me, it belongs to the one who conquered it. There's no knowing what he has in store for you."

As they travelled further, snow began to fall from the sky above. It was terribly cold, but it was also one of the most beautiful sights William had seen. He never imagined he would make it so far. Just up ahead, there appeared to be two figures on the road. One was small, the other was on horseback, and they were coming towards them. "Who're they?" asked William, struggling to see through the white haze.

The two figures resembled him and Noble. As they got closer, it became apparent that it was them. "I don't believe it," said William, "it's a giant mirror."

"No," said Noble. "It's a magic mirror."

The mirror was large and circular in shape, covering the width of the entire path. Its wooden stand was painted white, making it difficult to see. William watched as Noble walked up to the object and began to look himself over. "Spiders and frogs!" the dwarf laughed. "If only I had a bar of soap!"

"What do we do now? Should we go around?"

"Get off that horse," said Noble. "This'll be a real treat for you."

"Huh?" said William, quickly dismounting. He cautiously approached, "Wow! It's so clear! My armour looks beautiful!"

"Never mind your armour. I told you—this is a magic mirror. What would you like to see most of all?"

"See?"

"That's right. You can see anything you wish. Whatever your heart desires, you will see in real time," said Noble, backing away as William stepped closer to the mirror. "Well, what do you wish to see?"

"Krystal," he smiled. "I want to see if she's missing me."

Staring into the mirror, he watched it ripple and blur as an image began to appear—it was Krystal. She wasn't alone. William's smile faded when he realised she was with Gregory. "Are you sure this's real?"

"Yes, I'm afraid it is," Noble replied.

They appeared to be having a picnic in the woods. Gregory was cozying up to her as she flirted with him. "After all I've been through!" William growled. "It's not fair! My family's poor; Gregory's is rich! If not for his wealth, she wouldn't give him the time of day!"

"Do you wish you were Gregory?" asked Noble, with much curiosity.

William lowered his head, placed his hands on his hips, and let out a deep sigh. "No," he replied. "I know Gregory. He's not a nice person. He thinks he can buy people, like common goods. I'd rather be dead than be like him!"

"Well done, William," Noble smiled. "You've passed the sixth test. Because you've done so well, you may have one final glimpse in the mirror, if you wish?"

William watched as the image of Krystal slowly turned into his own reflection. "I'm afraid of what I might see..."

"This's your last chance to use it."

"Okay," he said. "I'd like to see Mary."

"So be it," Noble replied.

Again he watched as the mirror rippled and blurred into another image. William recognised Mary immediately, but something was wrong. She was at home lying in bed. "What's going on? Why's she crying?"

"Do you wish to hear her?" Noble asked.

"Yes!"

Her cries became audible. William watched as her mother entered the room and knelt by her bed. "My darling girl," she said. "He hasn't been gone for long. I'm sure he'll be fine."

"No one's ever made it back," Mary wept. "He's been gone for three days. He didn't take any food or water—I'll die if he doesn't return."

"I don't believe it," said William, "she's crying for me!"

"Does he know how you feel?" her mother asked.

"Yes, but he wants Krystal. I'll never be enough for him."

Before he could see more, the image began to fade. "Wait!" William cried, but it was too late—Mary was gone.

Staring into the mirror, tears began to flow from his eyes. "I didn't know she loved me so much… and I didn't know how much I loved her… until this very moment. I've been so foolish! Krystal? What was I thinking? She's not half the woman Mary is!"

"Krystal's very beautiful, isn't she?" asked Noble.

"Yes."

"The world often kneels before the young and beautiful. It sees what's on the outside, but not the deeper things; it cannot see the heart. Do you regret looking in the mirror?"

"No," William replied. "I can see things clearly now. If I ever get home, I'm going to run straight to Mary's house and ask her to marry me."

"She's quite a catch," said Noble. "Few men find a woman so loyal and loving. Then again, if I were in her shoes I may not be as forgiving."

"What do you mean?" he asked.

"How long were you chasing after Krystal?"

"Too long," William admitted.

"You'll have to be convincing if you wish Mary to overlook that fact. A woman's heart is a delicate thing; it can only handle so much pain before it turns to stone."

"You're right," he said. "I don't deserve a woman like Mary. But if I ever get the chance, I swear I'll make it up to her."

"We'll see…"

Chapter 11

The Stone Table

After making their way around the mirror, they continued their journey for many hours. William had no idea what his final test would be, but it was certainly taking its time to appear. Then, just up ahead, he noticed something odd.

"What's this?" he said. "A fork in the road?"

William waited for Noble to stop, then dismounted his horse. "Now's the time for you to choose," said the dwarf.

"Choose? You want me to decide which path to take?"

"That's right," said Noble. "The right path leads to death, and the left one leads to life. Choose wisely."

"Is this a trick? What's that?" asked William, pointing to a small, stone table, sitting at the junction between the two paths.

"This is no trick," Noble replied, "and it's not a test. The seventh test you will face, once you've made your decision."

"This doesn't make any sense. Who, in their right mind, would take the path of death?"

"Stand before each path—and choose."

William stepped towards the path on his left, which led to life. He felt a strange sensation, as if someone was expecting him to return from a long journey. With little enthusiasm, he stepped towards the right path, which led to death. As he stared down the snowy road he began to feel an even stranger sensation.

"I don't know why, but I feel that if I take the path of death, I'll find what I've been searching for my entire life. It feels a bit like home, or as if I've been separated from something—it's a longing I can't describe."

William turned to Noble. "Is Mary down there?"

"You know I can't tell you that," he replied.

"As weird as it may seem, I want to take the right path, but I don't think I'm ready."

"Is it to be the left one, then?"

"Yes," he smiled.

"You're going to be cold, but now you must remove your armour and sword."

"Why?"

"You're going on alone, and you must go by foot."

"But, Noble, I can't do this without you—you're my guide!"

Noble stared at him for a moment. "You'll understand soon enough."

With a deep sigh, William reluctantly removed his armour and sword, which took him about ten minutes in the freezing cold. "Okay, what now?"

"Go to the stone table and take what you find there."

He quietly approached. Standing before the table of stone, he saw something sticking up. It was covered in snow, but there appeared to be a large ring sitting on it. As he lifted it up, he felt a piercing pain in his fingers.

"Ouch!" he cried.

William watched as three drops of blood fell to the snow below. Shaking off the object, he was shocked to find it was a crown of thorns, covered in dry blood. Upon examination, he could see fresh spots of his own. "Is this what I think it is? How'd it get here?"

"Did it draw blood?"

"Yes," he replied, "three drops."

"Then put it back," said Noble.

With a deep reverence he placed it down, and said, "What now?"

"Now, you must take the path of life."

He turned to the dwarf. "Will I ever see you again?"

"That depends…"

"On what?"

"On whether you pass your final test."

William approached and extended his hand. "Goodbye, my friend. Thank you for being my guide. I wouldn't have made it this far without you."

"Good luck, William," said the dwarf, shaking his hand.

Noble's words were blunt, lacking emotion, which troubled him greatly. William had spent three days with the dwarf and had grown quite fond of him, despite their rough start. Yet, he was left with no other choice but to continue his journey alone.

He gave his horse a good pat, and waved Noble goodbye as he stepped onto the path of life. But after walking just a few feet he found himself in the middle of Geldirik. "Huh?" he said, turning around.

Behind him, William saw the rest of the town, including the sawmill in the distance. He glanced up and realised he had stepped through the old gateway, in the centre of town—the one they said was magic.

"It's William! He's done it! He's conquered the ancient path!" he heard a voice shout.

Looking around, he saw some of the townsfolk running from door to door, spreading the news of his return. "I don't get it…" he said, "I didn't complete my final test."

The air was cool; William realised it was almost dark. He noticed a large group of townsfolk coming towards him, smiling and cheering. For a brief moment, he felt warm and happy, as if he had been elevated above the clouds, but then he remembered what he had seen in the magic mirror.

"Mary!" he gasped. "Oh, I hope I'm not too late!"

With a huge smile on his face, he ran from the crowd, and didn't stop until he reached her house. After catching his breath he knocked on the door, which was answered by her mother. "William!" she cried. "I don't believe it!"

"Please, Ma'am, may I speak to your daughter?"

"Oh, she's upstairs. She's been very upset. I don't think she's ready to see you. Would you mind waiting a few minutes?"

"Please, Ma'am, it's very important," said William. "I've come to ask for Mary's hand in marriage."

She stood there in shock. "You've come to what? You took the ancient path because you wanted to marry Krystal, didn't you?"

"Yes, but the ancient path has taught me many things. I love your daughter a thousand times more than I could ever love Krystal."

"Well, then, you'd best get upstairs."

Chapter 12
The Seventh Test

With butterflies dancing in his stomach, William went inside and headed upstairs to Mary's bedroom. He stood outside the door and knocked. "Come in," said a soft voice.

He slowly opened it. "Mary?"

She stared up at him from her bed, and as her face lit-up with happiness, William could stand it no longer. He rushed to her bedside and wrapped his arms around her. "Oh, William!" she cried. "You've come back!"

Without letting him go she slowly sat up. He held her head and looked deeply into her eyes, which were filled with tears. "Mary, I have something to ask you?"

"Okay," she smiled, "but what happened? When did you get back?"

"I'll explain later, but right now I'd like to ask you something very important."

Mary could sense his passion. "Yes?"

William stood up and took a deep breath as he bent down on one knee. "You know I don't have much," he started to say, "and I've been so stupid these past six months, chasing after Krystal. I was blinded by her beauty, but now I see yours, and you're more beautiful to me than anything else in this world. I know I've hurt you, but I love you with all my heart. All I want is the chance to make up for it. Mary, will you marry me?"

"Oh, William!" she cried, throwing herself into his arms.

She kissed him deeply, then continued to kiss him all over the face. "I'm not complaining," he said, "but was that a yes?"

"Yes!" she laughed. "Of course it was!"

After telling Mary's mother, they left the house to inform William's. Many of the townsfolk had gathered outside his house, wondering where he had gone. Not wanting to make a spectacle, they snuck around the side. His mother had already heard the news that her son was back. She was keeping an eye out for him; and when she heard a tapping at the back door—she knew he has home.

"Oh, my boy!" she cried, seeing them together. "How did you survive? Are you hungry? You look so tired!"

They proceeded inside, but it was hard for William to breathe with his mother clinging to him. "Mother, I have something important tell you."

"Okay," she said, releasing her hold. "Mary and I are getting married."

She looked at Mary, who smiled at her. Completely overjoyed, they jumped into each other's arms, crying and laughing. William smiled, but was soon distracted by a noise coming from his bedroom upstairs. It sounded like someone shifting furniture. Then his mother turned to him, and said, "I have some news of my own, William. Your father's returned."

"My father! I don't believe it! Is he upstairs?"

"No," she replied. "He was wounded in battle, but everything's going to be fine. He was hit by debris from cannon fire, so he's at the hospital having a rest. We'll see him in the morning, but only for a bit."

William was overjoyed, but heard the strange noise again. "Mother, who's upstairs? I can hear someone moving about in my room."

They listened for a moment and heard a strange jingling sound. "There's someone up there alright," she gasped. "I hope it's not a thief."

"Perhaps one of the townsfolk climbed through the window?" said Mary. "They're very anxious to see William."

"Stay here," he said. "I'll go and see."

As quietly as he could, William made his way upstairs and approached his bedroom door. He pressed his ear against it, listening intently. There was nothing but silence. He cautiously opened it, and, sitting on his bed with a big smile on his face, was a familiar-looking dwarf. "Noble!" he cried. "What're you doing here?"

"Congratulations! You could've soaked-up all the glory from the townsfolk, but you didn't. Therefore, you have slain the dragon of earthly praise. You've done it, William! You've passed the seventh test!"

Hearing footsteps he turned around. "Mother, don't be frightened. It's okay, Mary. It's not a thief. This's my friend, Noble. He guided me along the ancient path."

Entering the room, they were shocked by his grubby appearance. "Good afternoon," he said, with a big smile.

"Hello," they both replied.

"It's great to see you, Noble," said William, "but what're you doing here?"

"Well, since you're the second person to walk the ancient path, and pass every test, I've left you a present in your wardrobe."

The dwarf was smiling but William was nervous; his journey had been full of surprises, and frankly, he was sick of them. With his mother and his future wife in the room to give him courage, he walked up and opened the doors. Like a dam of bursting water, shiny objects came ringing and pouring out.

"Gold!" they cried, watching it shine and sparkle as it filled the room.

Noble began to jump up and down on William's bed with laughter, causing Mary to join in. More and more gold poured out of the wardrobe, more than what could possibly fit—it was magic. As the room continued to fill, the gold was now up to William's knees. "Hey, I recognise that goblet—it's the dragon's hoard!"

"That's right!" Noble continued to laugh.

"We're rich!" William's mother cried, tossing some of the coins in the air.

As they examined the riches, Noble suddenly disappeared, never to be seen or heard from again. Not long after these strange events, William and Mary got married. Krystal was disappointed, but soon accepted Gregory's hand. As for the gold, William and Mary spread their wealth throughout the village, keeping a small portion for themselves. They lived long lives and had many children, all of which grew up healthy and strong.

At the age of seventy-seven, three days after Mary's passing, rumours reached William that a strange dwarf had been seen lurking around the ancient path. Whether they were true or not, didn't matter. William felt that he was ready to walk the ancient path again, to finally take the path of death…

The End...?